Matthew's
JOURNEY

Matthew's
JOURNEY

a novel

R.K. Johnston

TATE PUBLISHING *& Enterprises*

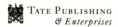
Tate Publishing
& *Enterprises*

Tate Publishing is committed to excellence in the publishing industry. Our staff of highly trained professionals, including editors, graphic designers, and marketing personnel, work together to produce the very finest books available. The company reflects the philosophy established by the founders, based on Psalms 68:11,

"The Lord Gave The Word And Great Was The Company Of Those Who Published It."

If you would like further information, please contact us:
1.888.361.9473 | www.tatepublishing.com
Tate Publishing & *Enterprises*, llc | 127 E. Trade Center Terrace
Mustang, Oklahoma 73064 USA

Matthew's Journey
Copyright © 2007 by R. K. Johnston. All rights reserved.
This title is also available as a Tate Out Loud product.
Visit www.tatepublishing.com for more information

No part of this publication may be reproduced, stored in a retrieval system or transmitted in any way by any means, electronic, mechanical, photocopy, recording or otherwise without the prior permission of the author except as provided by USA copyright law.

Scripture quotations marked "KJV" are taken from the *Holy Bible, King James Version*, Cambridge, 1769. Used by permission. All rights reserved.

This novel is a work of fiction. Names, descriptions, entities and incidents included in the story are products of the author's imagination. Any resemblance to actual persons, events and entities is entirely coincidental.
Book design copyright © 2007 by Tate Publishing, LLC. All rights reserved.

Cover design by Brandon Wood
Interior design by Elizabeth A. Mason

Published in the United States of America

ISBN: 978–1–6024712–5–8
07.02.05

This book is dedicated to Cary Jr., who is living proof of God's amazing, miraculous love. He, as well as his brother, J.B., was the inspiration for the content of this book.

To my wife, Emily, who has lovingly supported me throughout and has both inspired and stood by me in each and every facet of my life.

ONE

Matthew paused, for the briefest of moments, one foot braced against the tip of a massive boulder and the other planted firmly in place on the mountain peak. On a clear day one could see fifty plus miles in any direction. Today, however, Matthew could barely see the next summit protruding from the clouds. He could taste the moisture in the air; could smell it in his nostrils. His breath was thick in his throat as the altitude was making it difficult to breathe. The sting of the bitter western wind promised a dangerous cold front, and there would be no escaping the oncoming snow storm. Matthew glanced skyward nonchalantly. What did it matter? It wasn't like he was having a run of good luck. He had experienced one disaster after another in the last couple of weeks. The world seemed to have crumbled like sandstone beneath his feet.

He'd jumped into his car and had driven aimlessly, barely conscious of where he was going. His mind had ceased to reason. There was a longing in his soul as he searched desperately for something solid in his life to grasp onto, now only to find his dreams, his visions, and all the things he had taken for granted in his adult life, had vanished like vapor into thin air.

The night before he'd slept in his car, if sleep indeed was what you could call it. His heart ached from the constant worry he'd managed to burden himself with. At the first light of day he had crawled from his Saab and, in a state of complete confusion, began an ascent of the sprawling mountain in front of him. The tears that stung his then bloodshot eyes and blurred his vision had long since dried, leaving him emotionally spent, as well as physically exhausted. Was there anything left for him at home? Did he still have a home? Matthew's mind couldn't deal with it anymore. His head pounded from the mental overload that had pushed him over the edge.

The material things that had given relevance to his life no longer seemed to matter.

He had struck out up the mountain early on, catching the first rays of light as he ambled along the winding trail that led from the empty parking area. Climbing was something he had taken up only recently after a couple of interesting visits to an outdoor outfitter shop in Denver. Hiking and outdoor sports were some of his favorite things to do. They had a calming effect on him and he discovered it enabled him to forget his problems when he was alone with nature. He had purchased all of the ropes and hooks associated with climbing, along with a harness, but he barely knew how to use any of it. Luckily for him, he had without realizing it chosen a mountain that he didn't need a lot of skill with the ropes to climb. It was steep and time consuming, especially above the tree line, but until he got within a couple hundred feet of the top, it had been manageable.

That morning Matthew had climbed the mountain from its northern face and realized early on that he had bit off more than he could chew. The slope was steep, and the last two hundred feet or so had him scrambling over huge ice-covered boulders the size of his Saab, but he was far too stubborn and driven to give in and turn around. Besides, he was climbing with a nothing-to-lose attitude. He continued on, barely escaping bad falls a half dozen times before finally cresting the peak. Once at the top, he had fazed out. The climb had totally exhausted him. He was in good shape but not for the altitude at which he had been walking. He had managed to tune out everything on the way up, but his problems then seemed to have overtaken him in a bum rush as he became fatigued.

ଓ

Matthew began a slow descent from his lofty perch without motive or direction. There was only the sense in his disturbed mind that he needed to move. He picked his way down the rock-strewn mountainside like a zombie from a low budget horror film, from time to time casting a glance back at the peak behind him, which was becoming less and less visible as a heavy fog was starting to set in on the mountain tops. The fog was crystallizing into ice and making the surface of the terrain slicker and more treacherous as the day wore on.

He wondered about the name of the mountain he was on. Did it even have a name? The mountains were numerous in Colorado, and it would be easy for a man to lose himself in the vast wilderness and never be found again. The thought had crossed his mind more than once. A man could just disappear into the pines without a trace, live like a hermit in a land that was only miles from civilization, and as far as his family was concerned, there would be no one to ask questions.

There was a cornucopia of dirt roads that wound in and out of the mountains in the surrounding area and a plethora of trailheads that led to peak after peak. He had chosen one at random, not caring where his road might end.

Several hiking trails crisscrossed his, but each time Matthew ran across one of the beaten paths, he changed directions. He was not in the mood for company. Usually when he'd met people on hiking excursions, there was some type of friendly exchange. All he wanted now was to get away, not only from others, but from him-self as well. He was not unsociable, not in the least. His job had entailed entertaining people for hours each day.

Matthew was a shy young man when he began working at Jensen and Grobe, but had developed a sense of humor and a quick wit that had helped him to grow into his job. The clients seemed to love him, and the more they demanded having Matthew on their accounts, the higher his stock had gone with his boss. He had ridden high for a long time: confidence growing within him at every turn. But now he'd hit the wall and hit it hard. He didn't feel witty anymore. His self-assurance was gone, and only a shell of the man, remained.

Though he was usually cool under fire, he felt the poise that had exuded from him over the last ten years seep out like air from a balloon. It was a strange feeling for him, losing control as he had. He'd never even thought about it much, but it had seemed that in the past, he was always a step ahead of his problems. He had always been there to head them off and route them in another direction. He'd truly never needed anyone and had considered people that did to be weak.

All things come to an end, though, and in his hour of need he realized that he had not left the door open for anyone to help him. Now he needed a friend and in the worst sort of way. But there was no one for him to lean on. He knew he needed help. He hungered for it. But pride was a deadly monster that had come between him and everything he loved. Pride had sent him away into his own personal exile.

TWO

Matthew thought about the narrow, winding gravel road he had used to get to the mountain. Would it be closed in a severe snow storm? His was the only car in the makeshift parking lot that led to the trailhead, and no one knew where he was. Worse still, no one that knew him cared about where he was.

Nearly an hour later, with the peak behind him invisible among the low hanging clouds, Matthew simply sat down on a huge boulder with the cold piercing him to the bone. He stared into space for what seemed like an eternity; not as a man admiring the accomplishment of his climb up the mountain, but as a defeated soul. The weight of the world rested on his sagging shoulders. His head throbbed from a terrible migraine that made his eyes squint. His leathery face was suntanned from the time spent at Salt Lake the past summer, and he was beginning to take on laugh lines around his eyes and mouth that gave him an oddly tranquil appearance. Matthew was closing in on forty, although most people would put him at thirty-two or three. At six feet tall and around one hundred and ninety, he was in pretty good shape, even though he could stand to lose a few pounds. His dark hair was subtly starting to become speckled with gray; sometimes Kate, his wife, would razz him about it. Some of the guys at the office gave him a hard time about it as well, but he didn't care. Occasionally he found hair treatments on his desk but could never find the guilty party. He'd never been one to be self-conscious about his looks.

He was a leader in the office, and even though he didn't let it go to his head, he knew a lot of the guys looked up to him and valued his opinion. Kate at one time had been proud of him, too. She was always reassuring him and telling him what a good father and wonderful husband he was. He'd always thought that everything he did was for his family (or at least that's what he had told himself). Now he questioned his motives. Without them, what was there to strive for? He'd never thought of it in that context. Sure, he knew that a man was supposed to go out into the world and try to become the greatest and most important man he could be. To poke out his chest and say, "Look at what I've done." But when it all came down to it, what had he been doing? Providing for his family? Or was he just basking in his own glory?

CB

Time passed by in sheets of low hanging clouds that threatened to envelope him at any second. If only they could. At that moment he wished he could cease to exist. To just give himself over and lay down and rest for a while with no one wanting or expecting anything from him. He was content sitting there, his undershirt soaked with perspiration from overexertion, as fresh snow flakes randomly caressed his cheeks. Later, he would not be able to recollect how long he sat there. Only that time stood still. Never had he been as mentally and physically exhausted as he was in that instance. He could also never remember a time when he was so out of sorts. How could God, if indeed he did exist—and

Matt was beginning to have his doubts—create all of this and allow him to reach rock bottom as he had in the past couple of months? It seemed the roller coaster he had been riding had jumped tracks at a time when he had finally become comfortable with his life choices. Until recently he was at the top of his company in sales. There seemed to be no end to the free lunches. Kate and the kids were happy. Sure he and Kate hadn't been getting along as well as they once did. But he worked late hours to provide a good income for them so they could enjoy time shares in the Bahamas and weekends at Salt Lake. He was just too busy to see the signs. Now he was faced with the hard truth of losing it all. He had already lost Kate, and the kids, Evan and Rebecca, would be sure to side with her.

Then out of the clear blue, his company was shut down by the IRS, and all assets were frozen. He barely had enough notice to pack the things in his desk and get out. Although Matthew was not directly involved in any criminal wrongdoings, his company faced an investigation that could go on for years. His stock shares in the company were gone. His future finished. They would be lucky if they weren't sued by some of their clients, left in limbo.

Where would he be able to find a job? Although

he hadn't been charged with any criminal action yet, his clients would never be able to trust him again. Could he get at his retirement accounts? Since it was a 401k and opened through his company based on his earnings, he doubted it. All of those accounts were frozen. Would he have enough time to start all over? Could he rebuild his reputation? As he was climbing the corporate ladder, so did his lavish life-style. Along with that lifestyle came stacks of bills. He and his family's spending had spiraled out of control. He would have never suspected the end was so close. He had mentally told himself a couple of times, *All right after I buy this boat, this or that item, or one more trip to Vegas, then I'll slow down and pay off some things.* Matthew had never been able to follow through, though; always accumulating more. He lived as if there was no tomorrow, well above his means and recklessly out of his comfort zone. He rolled the dice and loved it! Lady luck, it seemed, had always smiled on him. As a result he began to feel more and more important, and Kate and the kids became less.

Kate had become so accustomed to her shopping sprees that she spent money at an alarming rate. He hadn't realized it at the time, but he had started her compulsive spending problem. He'd never known how deeply depressed she was. They had ceased communicating at that point, and the sad thing was he couldn't see it.

Life had all been about him at that time. His ego was over inflated, and he was unable to see the problems in their life. The problems that related to his work were all that he seemed concerned with. It had become too convenient to send Kate off to have her fun with friends whenever he had an agenda he wanted to pursue, such as a gambling trip to Vegas or a night out with the boys. When he did go on vacation with his family, he was there physically but detached from them emotionally. He always had a phone to his ear, dealing with problems at the office and waving his family off with his free hand for them to go on without him. Sure, he vacationed with them, but truthfully he never left the office. He had felt a little guilty from time to time but now the guilt weighed on him like a millstone. His life at that point had been purely materialistic.

He had come to the mountain defeated. All he wanted was to go somewhere and die. Then he'd thought about the contents of his pack. He tore the pack off of his back, fumbling at the zipper with his frozen, numbed hands. Inside he had found the instrument of his frantic desire. The nickel plated forty-five felt solid in his hand. He stared at it for a second as if it were the first time he'd seen it. Could he do it? He thrust the barrel into his mouth: his hand shaking violently now. The hot tears ran down his face and dripped onto the cold steel that stung his lips. His entire body shook: sweat beaded and stood out on his forehead. Fear gripped him and his stomach became a twisted knot.

Then just before he pulled the trigger, he snatched the gun from his mouth. He looked distastefully at the weapon. It was just a thing, not capable of doing anything by itself but an instrument of death when used correctly. He knew he didn't have it in him. He thought about his kids and how they would be affected. What kind of legacy would that be for them, if their father killed himself on a deserted mountain top? He was sickened by the weakness that had overtaken him. The thought chilled him to the bone. He wondered if it would be better if he just wandered off and died, never to be found.

He stood suddenly and threw the gun as far as he could. He watched as it skipped and bounced from rock to rock down a steep ravine: finally coming to rest in a crevice some hundreds of feet below him. His heart pounded in his chest, and his breaths came in ragged gasps. Only six months ago he had purchased the gun at a pawn shop for home protection. It felt like a cannon in his hand. Kate was furious with him. She strongly disagreed with having a gun in the house, but he'd been persistent with her until he finally won out. He wondered what she would think if he had killed himself. She had become cold and callous where he was concerned.

Matthew sat with his back to a boulder, his head in his hands, and shaking uncontrollably. Realism was beginning to set in. He was too prepared to give up, too ready to accept what had become of his life. He'd never been that way and detested the fact that he had let setbacks, no matter how great, take him down. The fact that he couldn't kill himself was proof that he wanted to live. He longed for the old Matt to take over. The Matt that was always cool under pressure. Surely there was a way for him to get back on top, a way to win back Kate and the kids and take his life back. He'd made it this far on nothing but determination and luck. "Never be a quitter," his grandpa had always said.

Matt was suddenly ashamed of himself. It was not like him to go crawling off somewhere licking his wounds and seeking a hiding place when the chips were down. He'd always stood up and stood up proudly to any opposition. Matthew felt a new surge of energy strengthening him. The old challenge was easing back. What was he scared of after all? He could get a job anywhere. His reputation in the business world might be tarnished, but he was prepared to overcome that obstacle. He surveyed his situation. One thing for sure was if he truly wanted to live, he would have to get off of the mountain before the storm hit. Then he could deal with his problems. He had been too wrapped up in his own misery. The realization began to set in that being trapped on a mountain in a bad snow storm, as unprepared as he was, was idiotic. He had come up here to die, expecting the elements to kill him if he found that he didn't have the nerves to do it himself. Now he knew that he had to get back down from this mountain to pick up the pieces and to right all of his wrongs.

Matt stepped out at a vigorous pace and with a new agenda. Focus had never been his problem. Direction, on the other hand, had. The weather was changing rapidly, and he was faced with a sudden decision. The obvious, quickest way down was to cross over and descend one of the hiking trails on the northwest side of the mountain, but that meant facing the oncoming storm. It was the fastest way down in good weather, but Matthew decided to stick with the southeastern side of the mountain, and even though he faced swirling winds, at least they weren't constantly in his face. The south side of the mountain also featured the least treacherous slope, with better footing. He also preferred hiking a longer distance in snow and ice on more level terrain than a shorter route over a steep slope in adverse conditions.

He needed to find shelter, and soon. Exposure at his present altitude could be deadly in just a short amount of time. His predicament was that if a storm set in, it could last for days or even weeks at that altitude. He'd seen what the Colorado blizzards were like, and he wanted no part of them.

In his haste, Matthew stumbled and fell, sliding fifteen to twenty feet down a draw. He caught himself on a boulder that jutted out about waist high, barely catching onto it with his left hand, and prevented another slide that maybe would have sent him plummeting down to the bottom of a deep ravine filled with jagged rocks. He pulled himself erect in the face of the oncoming storm, his eyes squinting hard against the wind to make sure he wasn't seeing things and trying to slow the drum of his heartbeat in his chest. He lowered himself slowly and scooted on the seat of his pants the remaining distance down the draw.

From where he had landed, only a few feet below him, was a makeshift trail along the edge of one of the cliffs, a trail that appeared to have steps carved out of the rocks in places. *Who would have made a trail here,* he wondered, *on such a narrow strip of soil that daintily hugged the side of the mountain?*

The trail was old, ancient, and if the truth was known, it was not a trail that had been used recently. When in use, it must have been heavily walked to still be worn as deep as it was. The soil up here was hard and the trail impression must have been a good two inches deep. He faintly remembered stories about an old land bridge trail that extended from north eastern Asia over the Arctic Circle and into North America. He had seen it on *National Geographic* or one of those shows the kids watched. He wondered if this trail could be as old. It was concealed by the lay of the land, and the narrow width of the trail made it almost imperceptible until you were right on top of it. He was sure that you'd probably be within ten or twenty yards of it on a clear day and never know it existed. Had it not been for his clumsiness, Matthew would have never discovered it.

Matt knew the local lore about the old Ute

Indians that had populated the area years ago. He wondered if they would have ventured this far up into the mountains. Perhaps they used the trail as a shortcut, or an escape route. The trail might have been hundreds of years old and would have been consistent with the Spanish arrival in the territory. Maybe it was used to flee from an army of soldiers. It would surely have been hard, dressed as the Conquistadors were in their suits of armor, to pursue the Ute up such a steep trail, and horses would have been out of the question. As Matthew stepped onto the old trail, he was instantly gripped by an eerie feeling. A cold chill ran up his spine when he thought about an ancient race of Indians coming up the steep face of the mountain. Perhaps they were waiting in ambush in certain spots, where the terrain favored the Native Americans. He closed his eyes and in his mind could hear the chanting, as single file columns would have slowly and methodically picked their way thousands of feet above the tree line. For an instant he thought he could hear the rattle of armor as soldier brushed against weary soldier in their pursuit of the Indians up a steep mountain slope. A slope that eventually would have left their horses thousands of feet below.

Matthew shook off the thought. He had always

been blessed with a vivid imagination. It used to get him into trouble in school and was a tool that had proven invaluable to him later in life. His ability to create often inspired sales gimmicks that managed to keep his company well ahead of the competition. He had always been complemented on his ability to "think outside the box," as his boss would tell him after sales meetings; where he managed to capture everyone's attention with his amusing presentations.

༄

The air was much thinner up here, and the trail was so narrow in places, a misstep in any direction could send him plummeting hundreds of feet. Footing was insecure at best in spots that featured loose shale. If indeed this was an escape route for the Native Americans, they had taken every advantage possible to keep the mighty Spanish army at bay. Field of vision was never more than twenty-five or thirty feet in any direction on the crooked path as it wound in and out of protruding boulders. To pursue someone armed, he thought, would be suicide. Matthew smiled and shook his head. He again conjured up images of a time long gone.

He descended a thousand feet or so on the

phantom trail before the sleet started to pound him. The footing was bad at best, and now the sense of urgency was on him. He had been about to give up only hours before, but now found the sense of survival welling up within him.

THREE

Almost as soon as the sleet started, the wind picked up. Visibility became near non-existent within minutes as Matthew plodded forward with his head bowed to prevent the frozen precipitation from stinging his eyes. The trail before that had been faint now was quickly becoming invisible. He had, as the sleet started, glanced down the mountain and found that he was only a good hundred feet above the tree line and angling down in a way that would have him there in minutes. The next couple of hundred feet beneath him leveled out to a much easier walking slope than he had seen since early that same morning. He scanned the trees for any sign of a place where he might hole up and wait out the storm. He might be able, he reasoned, to knock some branches off one of the aspens below and make a lean-to against one of the downed trees. He had almost reached the tree line when before him, as if unveiled by a magician, an outcropping of rock materialized. The sleet let up at that same instant, revealing the yawning mouth of a mountain side cave.

Matthew peered into the opening of the overhang to see if it would provide adequate shelter from the storm. *This is too good to be true,* he thought. He cupped his hands over his eyes, trying to adjust to the darkness that prevailed inside the cave. He was able to make out the back wall, or at least part of it. His new shelter was plenty deep enough to get him out of this storm and was a good break from the wind. The mouth of the cave, Matthew estimated, was as wide as a garage door, which tapered down considerably just under the overhang. At first he was wary of any critters that might be lurking inside of the welcoming maw of the entrance, but he soon forgot his fears as the cold began to sting his already pink hands. It was cold inside the cave, but there was no wind. Matthew looked around almost in disbelief. He might be stranded there for a while, and this would be his new home. This was his oasis to wait out the storm. Fuel was his first necessity. He knew that if he didn't find firewood, he'd probably freeze to death that night.

From the cave's mouth, he spied a pile of driftwood and headed out to retrieve it. The trek was much farther than he first realized. The going was difficult. He half slid, half ran, the remaining fifty feet or so to the tree line. He was unable to stop his momentum and tripped over a partially exposed log that sent him headlong into a brush pile. It would have been a nasty spill anywhere else, but as it were the old, dry, dead branches that would eventually serve to stoke his fire had gently broken his fall. He eased into a sitting position, and for a moment a hint of a smile played about the corners of his mouth. Maybe his luck was changing, he thought, as he sprang to his feet and began collecting wood, or maybe he had just been dazed from the fall. He laughed out loud at his reasoning.

Matthew turned and peered down the ever-increasing slope towards the tree line. If he had fallen another five feet, it could have been a much worse spill, as the mountainside dropped severely in front of him. Perhaps this was a good sign. It had been a long time since he had anything to smile or laugh about. As bad as his situation was, he actually was starting to enjoy it.

It was then that he saw the pack, or a part of it, anyway. He caught a glimpse of a dark green piece of canvas buried under years of leaves and brush. After a considerable amount of tugging, some precarious maneuvering of the brittle limbs and another near spill on the slope (which was becoming slicker by the minute), he managed to pull it free. So someone else had stumbled onto his hidden trail at some point in time; maybe not in the last year or so, but for sure more recent than its originators.

It was hard to imagine someone else stumbling upon this same route. He immediately wondered about the person who had lost the pack. Matt caught himself looking around, as if someone who may have lost the pack years ago was going to step up out of the trees and reclaim it. Again he had to laugh at himself for being so ridiculous.

The pack had weight, so he knew it contained something. But common sense for once overcame curiosity, and he threw it over his shoulder as he spent the better part of the next hour hauling load after load of wood up to his shelter in the rapidly deteriorating conditions.

The slope that led to his new winter home

could become treacherous within the next couple of hours and, depending on the heaviness of the snow, maybe hard for him to find from fifty feet away. However, as luck would have it, the sleet continued for perhaps another two hours before changing over to heavy snow. Matthew had by then already made a pot of coffee and eaten some beef jerky. He had purchased the jerky the night before along with some cheese crackers and little Debbie cakes at a store aptly named The Last Stop. The clerk, a young girl of maybe twenty-one or so, had looked at him with an interested smile as he continued to pile junk food on the counter. He of course had flirted with her a little as was customary with him. Looking back, he couldn't believe himself. There he was, obviously in a deranged state of mind, but still with the presence of mind to flirt with a young pretty girl. She had just laughed at him as she rang up what looked like a week's supply of unwholesome snacks. He remembered his college years and how he had lived off of coffee, beef jerky, and ramen noodles. He had vowed to never eat another ramen noodle, and he hadn't, but he actually missed the beef jerky and rarely started a day without a cup of hot coffee or two.

He wondered for the first time where he had left

his cell phone. The thing had rarely left his side in the last ten years. Although he probably couldn't even get service in such a remote area, he would have liked the opportunity to try Kate's number just to see if she would answer.

The weariness of the day finally set in, and Matthew lay back on his elbows, enjoying the warmth of the fire, and brushed against the all but forgotten backpack he had found during his skirmish with the unruly brush pile. He had dropped it off on the floor as he dropped his first load of firewood. He just never got back to it as he'd busied himself trying to get the semi-wet kindling burning. It had been nip and tuck for awhile, but luckily he had bought a good lighter the previous night at the convenience store.

Matthew tried to imagine himself attempting to scrape flint rocks together, or rubbing sticks together to start his fire. He remembered a story he had read many years ago about how the mountain men carried a leather pouch that contained two flint rocks to start their fires. *How pathetic we have become,* he thought. Years ago, families did a day's work around the house before he and his family normally got out of bed. Laziness was never a problem then, he suspected, as people had to do their part to survive.

He made a mental note that if and when he got off this mountain, his family would spend more time together and share in planned projects around the house everyday. They would move out into the country, he thought, and maybe have some farm animals. Evan and Rebecca were missing out on so much by not learning to take care of something that depends on you. He'd had that kind of experience on his grandfather's farm as a child, and it had taught him some valuable lessons.

Matthew struggled until finally getting some dry pine started. He had enough wood, he surmised, to last him for a couple of days or so. After dragging a heavy piece of aged hardwood on the fire and managing to feel warm for the first time all day, he pulled the old green canvas pack to him and began to go through its contents.

The pack had little that Matthew could use—a compass, which was a good one but was something he already possessed; an old metal canteen that would be put to use as soon as he could find a creek to wash it out; a small journal-like book that was half-filled with entries; and an old leather bound Bible that was nearly falling apart and soaked from cover to cover. Other than that, there were bits and pieces of snack foods and nuts that were long since past their prime and a shriveled up orange that was practically unrecognizable. Matthew laid the Bible along with the journal near the fire to dry and rested his head against his pack. Moments later he drifted off into the most untroubled sleep that he'd had in months.

FOUR

Dan Mason served as a park ranger for five years and had worked with the forestry for over twenty. He'd fought forest fires for the first eight years in these same mountains and fell in love with them as soon as he had seen them. Dan or "Big Dan," as most of his friends referred to the six foot four gentle giant, had the duty of riding through the parking areas for the eleven trailheads that wound in and out of the park each day.

The sleet, which had started an hour earlier, was really driving into the windshield now.

Dan looked at the outside temperature reading twenty-eight degrees. He was already late for supper today, and his wife had been cooking his favorite pot roast with potatoes, carrots, onions, and her special herbs. *Besides, no one in their right mind would be up there,* he reasoned, casting a glance at the fog-shrouded mountaintops that dominated the landscape. It was Tuesday after all, and a bad snow storm had been predicted to dump heavy snow on the peaks. Dan spun his new state-park-owned Ford F-150 into the north side trailhead and manufactured a neat u-turn just as he spied the black Saab turbo parked next to the trail info station. He made the same audible sigh that irritated his wife when she was fussing at him about something he had no control over. *Now why would someone ignore all of the warnings that had been posted about the upcoming storm and brave the elements,* he thought, shaking his head.

Dan pulled alongside the Saab and eased out of his truck. Maybe it was someone meeting a friend and just leaving their vehicle here, he hoped as he removed his work gloves and laid his hand on the hood of the black turbo. The hood was ice cold to the touch, and Dan grimaced a bit at the thought of anyone being a long way up the trail when the weather set in. He strained his eyes against the sting of the bitter western wind, as he followed the narrow little trail that wound off in the direction of the north peak. He hoped against hope to see someone weaving their way back to their vehicle in an attempt to get off the mountain before the storm hit. But there was no movement as far as his eyes could detect. The storm was predicted to last for several days and leave heavy drifts of snow on the higher peaks before subsiding. He remembered the forecast clearly as he peered through the hard little pellets of sleet that were now mixed occasionally with a few flakes of snow.

☙

While she was two years past her retirement, Martha Waters ran the desk at the State Park dispatch in Dothan. She was a wiry little woman that couldn't weigh a hundred pounds soaking wet, but with her sharp tongue and quick wit, she managed to win the respect of everyone that crossed her path. In a nervous voice, Dan had radioed to tell her of the car left at the north side trailhead.

She'd liked Dan the minute she'd met him over five years ago. He had a quick smile and friendly way about him. He had a way of talking to others that would make them feel that whatever they were saying was of the highest value. He made everybody feel important. He had, as a result of his friendship with Martha, been on the receiving end of quite a few batches of brownies over the years. He was very efficient on his job, and she liked his no-nonsense approach. So when Dan gave her the news of the abandoned car, it had troubled her, also. They had to deal with lost people on the mountains seven or eight times a year. In the past thirty years since she had run the service desk, more often than not most of these situations resulted in bad endings. She looked at her weather monitor again. They were going to get it this time for sure. The cold air and the moisture were going to bank in against the mountains and set in for a couple of days. Only thirty minutes earlier, they had posted warnings of blizzard-like conditions and possible whiteouts, with drifts up to three of four feet in the higher elevations. The thought sent chills up her spine that someone could be injured, lost or trapped up there. She forwarded the vehicle information that Dan had given her to both the local and state police agencies. All they could do now was, wait and see if someone was reported missing before they began a search of the mountains, and even then the helicopter couldn't fly in bad weather. She lowered her head and began to pray.

The phone still had a dial tone as Kate checked it for the fourth time. She'd been a nervous wreck all day. She and Matt had drifted apart, but she had never imagined them splitting up. To someone from the outside looking in, they seemed like they had it all—nice cars, nice boat, beautiful house with an in-ground pool and a guesthouse.

They were always going on vacation. She, Matthew and the kids went at least once a year on a cruise. They spent weekends—or at least she had—with the kids at Salt Lake many times in the last five years. She'd noticed the difference in him when he became "head of sales." He spent less time with them and more time entertaining the clients. At first, she was happy for him and proud because he had moved so fast in the company. Later, she became a little suspicious when he began entertaining female clients. Although she knew now that he had never been completely unfaithful to her, she felt sure that he had been at the time.

Matt was always putting her off, and she had gotten so lonely she began striking up a friendship with a co-worker, and although nothing happened with him, Matt had seen them out together. It had been a horrible scene, with Matt so outraged she thought he was going to attack the man. Her guilt had been constant since then, and she felt there would be no way to reconcile with him and that it was all her fault. Two weeks later his company had been shut down by the IRS. Details were sketchy, but to be sure, some people would face criminal charges. Luckily Matt wasn't involved, but still, just like that he was out of a job. He'd come home in a terrible mood that day, and they began to argue immediately. Bad went to worse, and soon they were at each others throats. Unfortunately Evan and Rebecca had witnessed the whole breakup, as the shouting match had reached a fevered pitch. Then as she was packing her things to go to her parents, he stormed out. That was yesterday, and she hadn't heard from him since. Only hours after their argument, she had tried to call him to apologize, realizing that maybe she wasn't sympathetic enough. He didn't answer his phone. They had never separated or stayed mad this long before, always making up within hours of any dispute.

The county police told her she had to wait twenty-four hours before filing a missing persons report, but she knew in her heart something was wrong. The pit in her stomach told her something was amiss. It was like Matt to storm out and avoid a fuss, but he usually came back within a few hours with a hangdog expression on his face, an apology, and a bouquet of flowers.

Kate had waited patiently for a while, having changed her mind about going to her folks, and cleaned house to pass the time. But like Matt, she wasn't a patient person either, and soon she was chewing on her nails and calling friends to see if they had spoken with him. No one had seen him for several days except for her and the kids. Kate looked at the clock as she grabbed up her purse and started for the door. It had been twenty-four hours!

༺ ༻

The young man holding down the phones at county post was two months shy of his twenty-seventh birthday. His boyish grin and shock of baby-white hair made him look like a teenager, a fact that at times annoyed him. He desperately wanted people to respect him, but unfortunately everybody in town knew him as "Little Willy" and refused to call him William or Corporal Johnson, which he really preferred. Next to the other deputies who were much his senior, he felt like Barney Fife, and they all treated him like a kid except for Parnell. Parnell was decent to him, and luckily they did a lot of night duty together. He was a tall, soft-spoken man that tended to defuse situations before they got started. William had learned a lot from Parnell. He had embraced Parnell's calming characteristics and learned from him how to remain cool during traumatic situations. There was something about Parnell that he hoped others saw in him.

He stared out the window that opened to a nearly deserted main street. He was bored to tears as he tapped out the Colorado Buffalos' fight song with his pencil on the desk. Sleet was beginning to pelt his cruiser, as they were just on the edge of a major winter storm. He had hoped he would be out of there and home before the storm set in, but that was not going to happen. His shift ended at twelve o'clock, and it was fifteen minutes after ten. He and Parnell were the only two at the northwestern command center, and with it being a Tuesday night, likely they wouldn't be needed. Heck, they weren't needed on Saturday nights. Not much happened in little towns in Colorado, and although he preferred it that way, it could get pretty boring. Oh, there were occasional bar fights and every now and then a traffic violation. But he'd only cuffed five people in the two years he had been there, and most of the time he knew the culprits. He and Parnell had carried more than one of his acquaintances home in the back of their cruisers on a Friday or Saturday night. More often than not he just sat by the radio, as he was doing tonight. He was waiting on reports from the other two cars that were owned by the tiny town of Harmon. The radio remained silent, however, and he had almost drifted off to sleep when the headlights of a silver blue Honda whipped in beside his Crown Vic cruiser. He sat bolt-upright as the lady hurried through the door, her eyes bloodshot and swollen from crying: her face a mask of agony.

He thought at first she had been beaten or raped, but as he jumped to his feet to help her, she motioned him back into his seat without a word.

"Are you all right Miss? He asked shakily, with a tone of genuine caring in his voice.

"I'm, I'm fine," she stuttered. "Its, it's just my husband. I'm afraid something has happened to him."

"Is he in some sort of trouble?" He asked as he pulled a pad from out of his desk. This would require some note taking, he was thinking.

"He didn't come home last night," she managed

with her voice beginning to crack. "I want to file a missing persons report."

"How long has he been missing?" William asked as he began thinking more like a cop than a concerned citizen.

"Twenty-five hours about fifteen minutes ago," she responded with a little cooler voice.

"Has he ever done anything like this before?"

"What do you mean?" She asked, beginning to become frustrated.

"Has he ever disappeared before or left without telling you where he was going?"

"No, never" she replied nervously. "He used to go on business trips and stay away for a couple of days at a time, but he always had those trips planned. Besides, he would always call me when he was away."

"Have the two of you had an argument?" William asked as he shuffled across the room to the filing cabinet, hoping they still had a missing persons form and he wouldn't have to call Parnell to the front.

The tears came again, and she wept aloud for a second. William was glad his back was to her. He hated to see a woman cry but knew he had to remain professional. He found the forms in the third drawer down and turned just as she found her voice again.

"We had a fight last night after supper and he stormed out. It was the worst one we've ever had," she sobbed as William offered her a Kleenex from the Captain's desk.

"Let's get his information down and get him into our system," William suggested. "We'll find him in no time. Now what's your husband's name?"

FIVE

Matthew awakened to a fire that had burned down to embers but was putting off a considerable amount of heat. It was his favorite part of a fire, the warm glow of the red hot coals late at night was always the best time to cook. It brought back memories of when he and his friends used to camp out when he was a teenager.

He missed those days of his youth that he supposed everybody at one point in time had to turn loose of, but you could never turn back the clock. He'd really like to change the last six months, or six years even, if he could go back and try to do things differently. To take some much needed time with his family and enjoy them instead of just living as greedily as he had over the last several years. Mathew had tried to supplement his time away from his family with material items, attempting to buy their love. His intentions were good, as good as any fathers. He'd wanted to provide for them more than anyone could ever know.

He knew now as he looked back that what he respected the most about his father was his ability, when the chips were down, to come through for his family. They never had much when he was a child. In fact, he couldn't remember many meals that didn't feature beans and potatoes. There were no expensive video games, no trips to the mall, no running the children from sport to sport as if he were a taxi service. Somehow, though, his father and mother had always shown their love unwaveringly. They always sat down to meals together, something that was rare in his household now. His father had made it a point to tell them often that he wanted more for his children than he had when he was growing up.

Matthew never comprehended how much his father had given of himself to their family. He remembered many times when his dad had come home from work so tired he would drop lifelessly into the easy chair in their living room. Matt and his sisters would come in excitedly, telling him about their day or what was going on around the house or in the neighborhood. He always seemed interested in what they were saying, Matt thought, even when it must have bored him to death. Matthew made another promise to himself; if he got his family back, there would be more communication and interaction between all of them. He would spend more time with his children and his wife. He would get to know them again. He and Kate had become so distant that they hardly knew each other anymore. She was more like a roommate that he never saw than a spouse. Even when they were pleasant to one another, it seemed rehearsed. They kept their dialog to a minimum while in front of the children.

He had blown it with her a long time ago. It wasn't her fault because she had really tried to hold it together. She tried to make time for the two of them, but he always managed to avoid the issue, and after a while, he just didn't know how to get back to square one with her. He was either busy at work or out with the boys celebrating having socked it to another client. Then he had caught her with the other man, and it destroyed him. He felt confident that everything was well in hand with her, that no one could ever take his place. He had really taken her for granted.

There they were in his favorite restaurant, making small talk and gazing into each others eyes over a bottle of wine. He had really shown out, too, charging in crazily and threatening the other guy when he was truly mad at Kate and himself. Then the next day when he braced her with it, she just shrugged and owned up to having been interested in him.

"I guess I was pretty lonely," she said coldly without even a hint of emotion.

And that was probably what hurt him the most—that she wasn't even fazed by the fact that he knew; that she had grown numb to their non-existent relationship to the point that cheating didn't even matter. It sent a dagger straight to his heart.

Hot tears poured down his cheeks once again. He choked down sobs and finally turned loose of his emotions in the face of one of the worst winter storms to hit that particular area of the Rockies in years.

ଔ

One look outside of the overhang told the story.

Even in the dark you could see how deep the snow was piling up around Matthew's shelter. It was a foot already if it was an inch, and the first inch of that was sleet. The temperature according to the thermometer on his backpack propped up outside of his shelter was twenty-two degrees. Any kind of movement outside would be treacherous considering the slope of the hillside, at least until some warmer temperatures came, and he wasn't sure of seeing that for a while. He wasn't even sure of how the weather was at this elevated altitude. He was sure the mountain was at least eight or nine thousand feet in altitude. He knew he must be fairly high on the mountain because he had just made it to the tree line. Matthew apparently would have to sit this one out for a while. He began to think of rationing his meager food supply, a problem that had not existed since his college years. Thinking of those days made him uneasy. At least, he thought, back then he could have asked someone for help.

Hours later, after he had drifted off into a deep sleep, Matthew awakened and found himself staring into the embers of his quickly dying fire. He sat there listening to the howling of the storm outside. He glanced at the old tattered Bible. It was still intact, but barely. Years had passed since he'd even picked one up. He ruffled through the pages to find it had thoroughly dried on the edges by the fire. It was, according to the credits on the front cover, a King James Version. On the inside cover was an inscription that read, "To Anthony Dodd with love, from Nana and Papa."

Some other inscriptions weren't as legible due to the smearing of wet ink, but appeared to pertain to birthdates and anniversaries. Matthew remembered as a child their Sundays and Wednesday nights in church. For years, he sang in the children's choir. Those days seemed like a world away for him now. There weren't many times when the church doors were open that his father didn't have them in the pews. Mathew tried to think of how long it had been since he had picked up a Bible much like the one in his hand now. He couldn't remember. The thought embarrassed him.

He began flipping to a scripture that always comforted him—Psalms 23: 4: "Yea, though I walk through the valley of the shadow of death, I will fear no evil: for thou art with me: thy rod and thy staff they comfort me."

He tried for an instant to hold back the tears. Matthew realized he had been trying to stand on his on. He'd convinced himself years earlier he didn't need anyone, that he was strong and could weather any storm, only to find himself here alone on a mountain and barely able to maintain his sanity. Matthew thought how he desperately needed that rod and staff. He bowed his head and, for the first time in years, prayed. He prayed as he had never prayed before. He hadn't been able to show his emotions to God as he did there on the dirt floor of that cold mountain cave, maybe he had never been pushed as close to the edge as he was. He opened his heart and rededicated his life to God with nothing but the cave walls, the storm, and the presence of the Holy Spirit to hear him. No burden so heavy was ever lifted off of a man's heart than was taken off of his that night, as the storm of the century raged outside of his shelter with all of its fury.

He remembered the story of how Jesus had calmed the storm that night on the ship when the disciples had awakened him fearing for their life. Suddenly he wasn't afraid anymore. The Devil had thrown everything at him and had succeeded in tearing him away from God for more than half of his life. Satan had destroyed everything he knew. Yet he still survived. Maybe with only the clothes on his back, but really, how much more did the disciples have when they ventured out to spread the good news? At some point after he had stoked up the fire, Mathew slipped off into a deep peaceful sleep.

He awakened to glowing embers and a faint lightening of the sky outside of the cave. The snow was still falling, although not nearly as heavy as it was during the night. The wind, however, had picked up, and the temperature was dropping fast. Matthew looked around his shelter, as if for the first time appreciating the size of the overhang. It was also much deeper than he at first thought, appearing to open into a corridor turning into the mountain. He would have to investigate that later on. The Indians that had found this cave had chosen well. For only time to time did he feel the bite of the cold wind that was raging against the Aspen-covered slope beneath him. Mathew bowed his head and thanked God for giving him shelter, fire and food in the face of the storm.

He glanced at the heap of supplies he had dumped out of his pack, and then retrieved the old Bible that lay near his feet. Matthew flipped to Romans 5:3–5: "And not only so, but we glory in tribulation also: Knowing that tribulation worketh patience: And patience, experience: and experience hope: And hope maketh not ashamed: Because the love of God is shed abroad in our hearts by the Holy

Ghost which is given unto us." Matthew marveled at these words. He had read them over and over again in his youth and had hardly understood them then. But now, looking back, he realized how problems in life can shape and mold you to be a better and more patient person. He had always been too spontaneous, too spur of the moment. Matthew never liked to wait on anything or anybody. It had been a fast moving world for him as an adult; a world filled with devices that made even the simplest chores a thing of the past. Life for Matthew had become too easy. He had become a person that he no longer recognized.

He remembered times when he had cursed someone while driving in his car for not moving out of his way fast enough. The thought embarrassed him now. It was a pressured world he lived in, he thought, and whenever he wanted something, he wanted it five minutes ago. Patience was not a word that could be used to describe Matthew. He read a few more verses in Romans and drifted off to sleep.

Some time later, when he awakened, the snow once again began to get heavy. He had never seen flakes as large as the ones falling at the mouth of his shelter. The fire had died down, and the fierce cold was now penetrating all the way to his bones. He quickly stoked up the fire and started another pot of coffee.

He cast a weary glance at the back of the cave. If he was going to stay warm, and if the temperature dropped much more, he would have to move his fire father back. He hoped when he did the smoke would exit as smoothly as it did where he had the fire now. Matthew's flashlight was deep in his pack, and as he fished it out, he tried to remember how old the batteries were. At least a year, he knew, but he could recall little else. The only time he had used it in the last year was when the power had gone out for about an hour during a summer thunderstorm.

The Mag light came on to his relief but was weaker than he'd hoped. He moved forward cautiously, maybe having watched too many horror movies, quite prepared to jump out of his skin, and not knowing what might have decided to hole up in such a grand cave during a cold Colorado winter. The cave made a slight turn from the entrance and opened up into a small cavern that was at least ten feet high. To his relief, he stood alone checking out a nearly perfectly rounded room.

From the inside, looking back to the passage he had entered, he could barely see the light from the cave entrance. The inside was much warmer than the sheltered ledge he'd camped on since yesterday afternoon. He once again glanced at the ceiling of the cave. Light peeked in from the top of the cave via a basketball-sized hole; he wondered if it would draw the smoke from his fire. His eyes went to the floor of the cave. In its day the cavern probably had seen many visitors. There were blackened coals from previous fires all over the cave floor, but it had been many years since the cave had seen its last visitor. Matthew dropped his pack and began dragging firewood back into the small room. He soon had his fire glowing and illuminating the walls that obviously concealed many stories of days gone by.

Inside of the cavern, the fire seemed much larger, casting huge shadows against the walls that danced and played in and out with each new avenue the flames took. Smoke filtered out the hole in the top of the cave nicely, and it only took minutes to completely warm the little room. Matthew glanced around again at the walls. There were hand holds cut out in one side of the wall that led from the floor of the cave to the top of the cavern. They apparently were there to enable someone to climb up and open or close the smoke hole, or maybe as an alternate escape route. He stepped outside again, his body thoroughly warmed for the first time in days. The snow was probably twenty inches deep and falling steadily, the temperature according to his pack was twelve degrees, and the wind was still whipping as it rocked and swayed the big aspen trees down the slope from his cave. He estimated the time to be around noon. His thoughts turned to his family as he pondered the predicament he had gotten himself into.

He wondered if Kate missed him. Did she even care? He knew Evan and Rebecca would be concerned.

"Oh, God," he called out!

How he missed them! He had never been that close with either of them, but everything he had done was for their welfare. Did they know that? Kate did. He knew she did, but she expected more out of him than that. She expected everything he provided and wanted more time with him than he was able to give. Would she tell them, he wondered, if anything happened to him. Would she tell them how much he loved them? She was a good mother even though they didn't see eye to eye.

Matthew ambled back inside and eased down beside the fire. His car had been the only car in the parking area when he set out on foot yesterday. And if they monitored the parking areas like they did in the state parks, a ranger had probably already run his tag number. They may or may not come looking for him, and if they did, it might take a week to get the search started. He retrieved from his pack a small, thick, gray book that looked as ragged and tattered as something he would expect to find in his grandmother's attic. His mother had stressed the importance of keeping a diary, and he had always carried one with him since he was a young man; the present one was his third in as many years. They were mostly filled with writings from his little excursions in the world of big business. He gently flipped it open and thumbed over three quarters of the way through until he reached the first blank page.

Matthew outlined the last couple of days. He held back nothing. He wrote as his old English teacher Mrs. Benson had taught him to write in college, with a passion. He wrote about the devastating losses he had encountered and his discovery of the old trail. He wrote about the backpack with the Bible, about his spiritual reawakening. He wrote about his love for his family, and he finally finished up with the weather and his current position inside the walls of the cave.

He glanced back over his diary when he was finished writing and then once again securely put it away. Matthew began stoking the fire back up as he enjoyed a warm pot of coffee, and still the snow fell.

☙

Darkness descended upon the mountain just as the snow began to turn into rain. The temperature had warmed up considerably towards the end of the day, and some of the snow had melted away; things were looking up. Matthew had spent the rest of the day inside by the fire reading from the book of Romans in the New Testament. He felt God's presence in his life for the first time since he was a child. *What a good, warm feeling,* he thought. God was in control of all things, and Matthew felt everything was going to be okay. He began to take stock of the supplies he had left and found he still had a pack of cheese crackers and a half dozen Slim Jims. He ate a half of a Slim Jim and two cheese crackers, deciding to ration himself in case he couldn't strike out for home the following day.

Matthew dropped his head and gave thanks for his existence, for God showing him the way to the cave, and for providing all things including hope in his time of despair. Matthew declared that life was going to be better when he got home. It wouldn't be easy, he knew. There would always be pitfalls and vises out to snare him, especially since he had made a pact with himself and God to be a better person. There would be traps laid cunningly by the Devil, who always seemed to know his weaknesses. He would have to keep his guard up and his senses alert. Matthew knew if he didn't, he would find himself slipping into his old ways again. A new sense of excitement filled him and elevated him to a level he hadn't experienced in some time. Matthew couldn't wait to get home and begin his new life. He just knew that God had something good planned for him.

He awoke some time in the middle of the night with the fire dying down to dull glowing embers. Somewhere in the night a wolf called a long way off. He lay there listening to the mournful sound fade away, and then there was quiet. Something was missing from when he drifted off to sleep. He lay there for what seemed like forever, but was in reality for only a few minutes, trying to figure out what was troubling him. Finally it dawned on him, the silence. There was no wind whistling outside and no drip, drip, dripping of the melting snow falling from the outside roof of the cavern. After dropping a couple of fresh sticks on the fire, Matthew stepped outside to survey his situation.

A full moon illuminated the steep slope in front of him, casting eerie shadows on the shiny, ice-covered slope. Yes, ice-covered. The rain had fallen and melted maybe half of the snow, but now the top two inches was nothing but a solid sheet of dangerous ice.

There would be no leaving tomorrow unless there was a miraculous thaw, and even with that, it would take hours for the ice to completely melt off. Matthew eased back inside and sat by the fire once again. He had enough food to last another day, and that was rationing it. If he was stuck up here another two or three days, he knew he would be getting terribly hungry. The firewood he noticed was also getting low. He knew he could survive without food, but the warmth of the fire he desperately needed. He remembered the "rule of three" when in severe weather. One can survive three weeks without food, three days without water, and only three hours without shelter. Come daybreak he would have to try to round up some wood to keep his water supply melted and his body warm, which meant he would have to take his chances on the slippery slope in front of his cave. Then the wood would have to dry in front of the fire before it would burn. Matthew slipped off into a troubled sleep, his faith faltering and shaken.

SIX

He awakened to a brilliant glare. The sun was up and reflecting off of the ice-covered landscape with amazing clarity. Had it not been for his predicament, it would have been one of the most beautiful sights he had ever seen, but unfortunately, under the circumstances, he was forced to not like it very much. The sun could only be that bright for one reason; there were no clouds. He knew at his present elevation, clear skies combined with snow and ice could mean dangerously cold temperatures. Matthew stepped outside. He was not disappointed in his calculations. The thermometer read minus five degrees—the coldest temps he had ever seen.

He surveyed the slope in front of him. An idea had gone through his mind early that morning about how to safely get firewood without taking a bad spill on the hillside. He had planned to secure his grappling hook inside the cave and lower himself to the brush pile, chip away at the ice with his pick and tie the wood to his rope. Then he would pull himself up to the cave by the rope, and once inside would pull the wood up behind him. The plan made even more sense with the slick ice covering everything. Matthew smiled, very much pleased with himself. *It could work,* he thought, and he began pulling out his rope.

There were many places inside of the cave mouth to secure the grappling hook. Several hulking boulders were at the front of the cave, which he could use. Matthew chose two likely ones that jutted out from the cave entrance, and after he had wedged and tied it off, he threw his pack over his shoulder and began the treacherous descent down the icy slope. Footing was impossible, as Matthew discovered before he had gone far. He spent most of the time on his belly sliding down the hillside, feet first, clutching his rope.

When he finally reached the brush pile, there was still about twenty feet of rope paid out behind him. Reaching into his pack, he fumbled for his pick. The grip he had maintained on the rope and the bitter cold made his hands so numb that he had to work his fingers for a minute to get the feeling back. He picked and chipped at the frozen logs until he had three nice ones loosened. They were each about seven to eight feet long and would provide enough fuel to last for another day or day-and-a-half at least. After he had them in his cave, he would chop them up with his hatchet into burning size. He looped his climbing rope around them until they were positioned firmly and tied them off. The cold by then had penetrated every part of his body. The parka that had kept him at least comfortable through most of his journey seemed to be of almost no help at all now. His feet were like ice, and he could barely feel his toes. He'd kept his face covered as much as possible but now could feel the sting of the cold on his skin.

He turned to take a step up the slope and reached out for the rope, but as he leaned over, his hands didn't work for a second. They were clutched arthritically; he found himself grabbing for the rope but unable to grip it. In that instant his feet went out from under him, and there was a desperate moment when he was reaching for anything and catching nothing but air. He fell backwards down the slope.

The first five feet or so were straight off before turning into a roller-coaster-like hillside. Matthew hit with a thud that jarred his teeth and then went careening down the slope, grasping and groping for anything that would slow his fall. There was nothing but ice covered landscape and little to grab on to. Matthew was at the mercy of the slope until he hit the trunk of a large aspen tree. He hit the tree feet first and then almost stood straight up, as his head caught one of the lower branches. His world spun. He was vaguely aware of splitting pain in both his legs and head. Then there was darkness.

☙

Matt came to just a few minutes or so later, but to him it could have been hours. He found himself facing downhill and leaning against a monster of an aspen tree that he had crashed into as he rocketed down the slope at breakneck speed. He sat for a long moment in the bitter cold, like a prize fighter that had been knocked out of the ring, not knowing who or exactly where he was. Fortunately, with each passing second, some of the cobwebs were going away and he was becoming more and more aware of his surroundings. As he did, however, panic began to set in. His head throbbed with pain. He reached up to his forehead and immediately discovered a gash about three inches long and fairly deep. Blood was all over his hand, and he realized it was running down the side of his face. The snow around where he sat was stained dark crimson red. The limb he had hit was now colored with his blood, as well as his pants and boots.

The slope in front of him dropped off rapidly. The area he had fallen from was steep, but if he had continued another fifteen yards, he would have dropped off the edge of the world. A cliff lay straight in front of him. Matthew couldn't see the drop from where he sat and didn't want to see it either. What he could see was the vast emptiness that was open air where a stand of trees should be.

Matthew shuddered as the cold started to reach him. He lay still for a few minutes and a few minutes would be all it would take in such frigid weather. Men had frozen to death in better conditions, Matt knew. While looking back to see if he could see his cave, the urgency was in him to move and move soon to some protection. He spied his rope some thirty feet up a tricky incline from him. It would be thirty dangerous feet, he thought, as he half-turned again and looked at the great chasm before him, but the only other option was to sit there and freeze to death.

Matthew spun around and, in one motion, while holding on to the trunk of the great aspen, attempted to pull himself erect. White hot pain shot through his body, Matt's vision blurred, he looked down at his left leg that had collapsed against the mighty tree as he had attempted to rise. A few crucial seconds went by as he very nearly passed out again. Hot bile arose in his throat, and he felt he would lose the contents of his stomach. One look at his leg told Matthew all he needed to know. It was broken below the knee. The bone wasn't sticking out, but his leg was canted over at a funny angle, and he needed no doctor to tell him the prognosis.

Matthew realized if he were going to get back to his cave, he would do it without the use of his bad leg. He searched his pack shakily and found his hatchet. Now if he could only locate his pick, he could use the hatchet and pick to pull himself up the slope, hand over hand until he reached his rope. After a brief search, he located his pick; it had been in his hand as he fell and now lay some distance away on the other side of the tree from him. The retrieval of the pick was uneventful but time consuming as he crawled, dragging his left leg and chopping out with the hatchet into the ice. He began pulling himself along inch by inch. Once he had the pick, he surveyed the hillside in front of him. The shortest way back was obviously the way he had fallen, but it was also the most dangerous. There was a gentler slope in the direction where he had dropped his pick, and he immediately struck out.

Twenty minutes later, he was completely exhausted and only halfway to the end of the rope. The going was hard, and the hillside turned out to be even steeper than it had appeared. Matt discovered that as he tired, he could only move about six inches at a time, and when he reached out farther with his pick and hatchet, he didn't have enough strength to pull himself up to them. He lay there, face buried in the snow and ice, defeated and broken. Matthew closed his eyes and prayed for strength, realizing once again he was trying to make it on his own. He knew if he didn't keep moving, he was only minutes away from death.

He took a deep breath and raised his pick, driving it deep into the ice and pulling himself forward in the same motion. Then he did the same with his other hand. Pretty soon Matt had a good rhythm going, and in no time had brought himself to his rope. He stashed the pick and hatchet in his backpack and began pulling himself back up the icy ravine, finally stopping at the brush pile that had caused his fall. He was exhausted, and even though the temperatures had hovered around zero all morning, he was covered with sweat from head to toe. The altitude and slope had him sucking wind so hard that his side hurt. He knew, however, that he couldn't have made it as far up the ravine as he had if it weren't for some divine intervention. Six months ago, if someone had spoken of divine intervention, he would have thought them foolish. Not any more; he would never take God lightly again! He stopped long enough to give thanks to God for allowing him to reach the rope.

Matthew pulled himself along until at last he reached his frozen fire logs. His hands were cramping so bad he could barely open and close his fists, so after a short rest and a breath of air, Matt took off his gloves and began wringing his hands to try to get the circulation back. His hands were pink from the bitter cold, and he wondered if his face and feet looked as bad. The breath was coming out of him in ragged gasps, and his throat was raw from breathing in the frigid air.

Life seemed precious to him in that instant there on the icy slope. He realized he might never get off of the mountain now. Matthew's leg throbbed, and he had dragged it painfully the whole time. He chanced a glimpse at it once more, hoping his injury wasn't as bad as he previously thought. The leg was turned in at an angle that wasn't normal. The sight sickened him, and for a moment he wished he hadn't looked. A Bible passage came to him as he lay there catching his breath: "I'll never leave you nor forsake you."

Matthew knew in that instance he wasn't alone. The thought energized him as he grabbed the rope and once again began his ascent towards the cave. The opening of the cave was a welcome and comforting sight. He managed to drag himself inside with the last vestiges of his strength. The only thing he was aware of before passing out was the terrible pain in his leg. The walls became a blur and he slipped into unconsciousness, awakening, periodically only to look around a room that was spinning out of control. With consciousness came a terrible motion sickness, and a feeling of drunkenness came over him.

He lay awake staring into the still hot coals of his fire, not yet comprehending all that had happened to him and the pain he was feeling. Any movement sent waves of excruciating pain throughout his body and sickness to his stomach. Matt managed to pull his canteen to him and took a deep swig of water. It made him feel better, but that wasn't saying much. He apparently had more problems than just a broken leg and a bump on his skull. Chills seized his body one minute, and the next he was soaked in sweat. Exposure had done something to him. Maybe, he had even succumbed to a light stroke, he thought. He closed his right eye and discovered he could see out of his left, but it was blurred. He had a long scrape down his right arm where he had hooked a jagged rock as he tried to slow his slide. The gash on his head was only about three inches long but was very deep, and he was covered in blood from it. His leg told the tale, though, with it being in the shape it was.

I might never get out of here, he thought.

CB

He heard the thumping in his ears minutes before it registered in his mind—a familiar sound, although in his state of semi consciousness, he couldn't quite put his finger on it. His eyes fluttered open for a minute, catching the blinding glare of bright sunlight off of the ice. The thumping sound was beginning to fade just as he recognized its origin. It was the sound of helicopter rotors. He turned toward the entrance of the cave and half raised himself against the wall in a feeble attempt to pull himself erect. Only his strength had left him. He slid down the wall into a sitting position, and as the chopper faded into the distance, he slumped on the floor of the cave, helpless and unable to rise.

SEVEN

Roger Stuckey kept his Bell OH-58 at a comfortable height above the peaks and flew in slow, arcing circles to allow Ranger Mason to scour the mountainside for the missing man. He'd flown a half dozen times on searches as a favor to Dan, but never when the weather had been as bad as this. *This Matthew Brogan must have been crazy to come up here in such a bad storm,* he thought. If Dan hadn't been one of his closest friends, he would not have flown today. All morning he'd entertained the idea of a hot cup of coffee and a doughnut at Chelsea's on 5th Street.

"Like finding a needle in a haystack," he offered over the thumping of the rotors.

Dan's face remained glued to the window and appeared transfixed to the landscape below. Dan didn't respond, and Roger knew instantly he was a little peeved at him. Dan practically had to beg him to go out today, and he felt a little bad about it, realizing that if he were in trouble, Dan would be the first to come looking for him. He also knew that Dan was a good man and that he felt somewhat responsible for finding the man that was missing on his watch.

This was Dan's backyard, and anything less than a thorough search would be inexcusable for him. He had put the big man off for nearly twenty-four hours, not just because he didn't want to fly, but the wind gusts in the peaks were too strong. *There was no way,* he thought, *that a man could survive the conditions on the mountain.*

"Make another pass," Dan motioned without looking at Roger, indicating the north side of the mountain where the man's car had been found.

"Another weather maker on the way tonight," Dan offered without emotion after a long pause.

He still stared at the landscape intently as the Bell banked smoothly and slowly. They trolled at a comfortable altitude above the snow-covered mountain pass.

"Drifts are too deep," he said more to himself than to Roger.

"We're going to have to take her back home Dan," the OH-58 pilot said nervously as a strong gust swayed the helicopter.

The winds were picking up. Roger took her up another hundred feet. Dan had started to argue, but he knew that Roger was right. He'd felt the bird rocking for the last few minutes, and though he knew that Roger was the best pilot in the area, nobody could hold it steady in those severe winds. He owed Roger one for asking him to fly under such adverse conditions.

"Turn her around," Dan muttered, still staring at the frozen landscape below as another strong gust shook the chopper. There was no use putting their lives in danger as well. "I'll buy you a cup of coffee when we land," he offered.

Roger smiled. He was relieved Dan wasn't mad at him.

The OH-58 banked steeply to the southern side of the mountain and skirted the area one more time. If he was still alive, it would be a miracle. *No man could survive the temperatures that this Matthew would face tonight,* Dan thought, *at least not without some form of adequate shelter.* He continued to press his face against the cold glass in an attempt to get one last look at the mountain as the chopper sped for home.

○§

The doors to the old 19th century church where she and the kids had been members for the last two years opened easily under the gentle pressure of Kate's hands. She wandered down a dozen pews or so before sliding into one of the seats. No one was in sight as she bowed her head. She realized she could pray anywhere, but here she still felt more at peace, and more in the presence of God than she did at home. Matthew always found an excuse to not go to church. He would say that he would go next week or another time, but next week never came. She found herself praying that God would protect and move in his life. She had never felt as helpless as she did now. She didn't realize how much he had become a part of her. Now something was missing, a vital piece of her life.

Her whole heart and soul was in the prayer, as the tears once again began to flow down her cheeks. She opened her eyes and raised her head while fishing in her handbag for a tissue. Pastor Jones had silently come in from one of the Sunday school rooms and was smiling at her comfortingly. He had kept his distance respectfully. He fumbled with some papers on the altar, trying to look as preoccupied as possible in his non-assuming way. The nearly seventy-year-old pastor had a way about him that instantly put you at ease. Kate had liked him immediately. He was always understanding to everyone's problems and quick to lean an ear in their time on need. He made her feel like a chosen child of God, no matter what she was going through.

His kind eyes met hers, and after deciding he had given her time to pull herself together, he began to slowly walk in her direction. After exchanging a few moments of pleasantries, she quickly broke down and began telling him about what had happened. He just nodded, comforting her and assuring her that God is in control of all things and that He is a God of mercy and grace. He then took her hand and began to pray that Matthew would be sheltered and blessed by the Lord. He prayed that angels would watch over him and keep him safe and warm. It was a beautiful prayer and it lifted her spirits tremendously. She hugged him, immediately feeling better.

When she returned to her car, her cell phone

was ringing. Dan Mason was on the other end, and he related that they had to break off the search early because of the weather conditions. They would try again tomorrow, he promised her, if the weather permitted. She thanked him and, after a long sigh, started her car and headed for home.

○○

Consciousness returned along with the pain for Matthew. The coals of his fire had burned dangerously low. Matthew dragged himself across the cave to the dry pine he had managed to procure the day before.

He got the fire stoked back up and burning within minutes. The cave had gotten cold in the time he had been unconscious. He could only imagine how cold it must be outside. He had to face the facts that he would soon have to go out and drag up the wood that was still tied to the rope and pull it into his cave. He chanced another look at his leg. The bone was not protruding through the skin, but it was obviously broken. His leg below the knee was canted at a funny angle.

Matthew reached for a piece of dried hardwood and selected one that was about as big around as his wrist. After chopping it down on the end to about a foot long, he cut the straps off of the backpack he had found and tied the stick to his leg above and below the break. He cut another stick the length that he would need to use for a crutch. It had a nice fork at the top that allowed his armpit to sit comfortably in the notch. Matthew tried it out around the inside of the cave. *It would work,* he thought, *if the temperature warmed and some of the ice melted.* It was a long shot, but he might be able to walk out of there.

Outside the cave entrance, the temperatures had dropped even more since morning. As soon as he had stepped out of the entrance, the cold stung his face. He began to tug on the rope using a short deliberate motion. As he pulled a little, he would wrap the rope around a large rock at the entrance. It was a struggle to get leverage without the use of his bad leg. After much difficulty, he dragged himself inside the cave to warm up. He hadn't realized how exhausted he had become. His head dropped and he began to pray. "Lord God, give me strength," he prayed. "Forgive me for not trusting you more. I pray that wherever my family is or whatever they are doing that you will bless them and strengthen them. In Jesus' name I pray, amen."

He had no idea that at that same moment, Kate was pouring her heart out in a church some forty miles away on his behalf, and that a preacher would be on his knees that same day asking for his safe deliverance. He couldn't foresee a forest ranger named Dan Mason talking to God later that night and pleading his case. All he knew was that after a few minutes of rest, he arose with renewed vigor and, without even thinking about it, began pulling the wood up the remaining portion of the slope. Soon he had it in front of the fire drying while he began to make a pot of coffee.

The next storm came in with a fury. The wind whistled and moaned as he huddled inside the cave around his fire. Even though the cave was toasty, chills racked his body. He pulled the Bible out of the pack and flipped it open to Psalms 69:1–3. Matthew read aloud as he suddenly felt akin to the author's peril. "Save me, O God," it said. "For the waters are come in unto my soul. I sink in deep mire, where there is no standing: I am come into deep waters, where the floods overflow me. I am weary of my crying: My throat is dried: mine eyes fail while I wait for my God." He felt those verses penetrate into his soul. He had never read anything that reached him as the Psalmist's words had.

The author had of course been King David, and in accordance with the rest of the chapter, he had been in peril from his enemies. For God, Matthew remembered, had loved King David and referred to him as a man after his own heart. He also knew that the much beloved King had shattered basically all of the Ten Commandments. God was a God of forgiveness, however, and as he read through the Psalms, it was obvious that King David cried out to God for mercy on many occasions. Psalms 69:13 read "But as for me, my prayer is unto thee, O Lord, in an acceptable time: O God, in the multitude of thy mercy hear me, in the truth of thy salvation."

Matthew closed the Bible and began to pray again. This time he recited the twenty-third Psalm. He had learned the prayer by heart when he was thirteen years old at vacation Bible school, and it stuck with him. Incredibly, it hadn't meant that much to him at the time. *You could never understand the pains that you go through sometimes daily as an adult,* he guessed, *when you were a child.* His parents had sheltered him considerably, and he hadn't wanted for much as a young adult. His soul hungered now, though, for comfort that couldn't be given by human hearts.

Sleep claimed Matthew at some point, and

dreams of better times played through his mind. His family was once again together, walking hand in hand on a warm, tropical beach. In his dream it was early morning; the sweet salt breeze ruffled his hair. Seagulls squawked overhead, and sandpipers ran to and fro, occasionally digging into the sand for some unseen morsel. No one talked in the dream, the kids were much younger and Kate looked at him the same way he used to catch her looking at him when they had been close. Matthew awakened abruptly as the fire crackled and popped. He looked down at the Bible that had fallen into his lap open to the Gospel of John. One verse of chapter fourteen was underlined, verse sixteen. "And I will pray the father, and he shall give you another comforter, that he may abide with you forever." He stared at the words for a moment and knew that he was in God's love and favor. Some bad things had happened to him but, he realized, his situation could have been much worse. He had, of course, found the shelter of the cave and had at this point remained warm and safe even through a terrible accident.

He moved to get up, and pain shot through him like an electric current. His leg had rested at a funny angle while he slept, and the cold had stiffened it considerably. Matthew knew he was going to have to leave as soon as the weather broke if he was ever going to make it off of the mountain. His meager supply of junk food was running out, and he felt his body getting weaker. The sound of water dripping caught his ears as he gingerly touched his mangled leg. He made his way to the cave entrance, leaning against the wall. The morning sun gleamed off the snow like stainless steel. The surprising warmth of the morning air caught him off guard as he approached the entrance to his lair. Apparently, sometime in the night a warm front had passed through and the snow was quickly melting, sending little rivulets of water down the face of the slope.

EIGHT

Matthew made his decision then and there. The ice had thawed quite a bit during the night and revealed soft snow beneath. This might be his one chance to make it out, and his window of opportunity could be very small. He threw his newly found Bible and what remained of his cheese crackers into his pack. Then he pulled out his journal and began to write: "Kate, Rebecca, and Evan, if you find this journal, it will probably mean that I did not make it back. I want you all to know how much I love you. My leaving was a terrible mistake and I realize that now. Please know that because of this error, I have found a peace with God that before I could have never known." Matthew stared at the journal, realizing that this was perhaps the last communication he would ever have with his beloved family. He sat calmly for a moment in a tranquil state, thinking only of them. Finally collecting himself he searched for a safe harbor and placed his journal inside a deep crevice at the back of the cave, where it would be easily found. He retrieved the crutch he had made and, after a brief prayer, began his descent down the treacherous mountainside. The going was extremely slow, and each little slip brought a new stab of pain to his body. Matthew was not disillusioned; he knew that if he didn't make it off of the mountain during the day and couldn't find a place to hole up, he would probably freeze to death that night. It was a chance he would have to take. Either freeze or starve. And as long as God gave him the strength to move he was going ahead. Just as Paul had described, he was more than a conqueror; he would press forward.

Within the hour Matthew had to stop for a rest. His breath was coming in ragged gasps, and his back was already hurting as he overcompensated for his leg. He looked over his shoulder at his back trail in dismay; he hadn't covered much distance at all. Although he couldn't see the mouth of his cave, he recognized the rock formations around it. "God give me strength," he muttered half under his breath as he once again started out, pushing off with his makeshift crutch.

Two hours into his flight, he'd become so accustomed to the pain in his leg that he didn't even wince anymore when he put weight on it. Instead he became acutely aware of his other aches and pains, like the gash in his scalp and the throbbing headache that accompanied it. He tried to picture himself with his family, happy and safe. He only hoped he could get back to that point, but at this time it seemed like a different world.

Again he pressed on. Although his pace had slowed somewhat and he didn't have the urgency in his step, he plodded slowly and methodically onward down the still slick but ever-improving slope. He had at least gotten well into the tree line, where he was able to catch himself and prop against the base of a tree from time to time. The sun was high now, and the snow under Matthew's feet had turned to slush. For over the last hour, he noticed, the slushy snow had soaked him almost to his knees. He wanted to stop to rest, but no, that was out of the question. He couldn't give in now! To give in would be to give up, and he refused to stop. He continued on, half dragging his body down the slope.

Within an hour the hillside leveled off and the walking became easier. Matthew finally pulled up at a boulder and leaned against it for a short rest. His head ached as did his leg and a myriad of other places in his body. He was still pretty high up, he reasoned, for the land to be as level as it was. At some point, he thought, he would have to encounter more sloped terrain. A bad feeling came over him that he couldn't explain. The urgency to get up and move, to press on, took over.

Something was wrong, bad wrong. He limped in desperation forward in the direction that should have been down hill. A level plain remained in front of him as he limped faster and faster, suddenly realizing where he was, and then just as he had known it would be, it unfolded there before him. A gaping abyss opened before his eyes. The flat terrain he had been walking abruptly stopped at sheer cliffs. He had in his urgency to get off of the mountain walked down a hillside and out onto a plateau.

The towering cliffs dropped off in front of him at every angle. His heart sank in his chest. Matthew's eyes took in the hillside behind him. In order for him to get off of the plateau, he would have to hike a ways back up the mountain, and then cross another ridge horizontally to get to a place where he could begin his descent. Tears of pain and failure welled up in his eyes. He knew he couldn't make the hike back up the mountain, and even if he could, it would probably take hours. And hours were a commodity he no longer possessed.

Physical exhaustion and mental anguish converged to drag him to the ground. He had given it his all and had nothing left. He bowed where he was, with one knee on the ground and his bad leg stretched out, to pray one more time to God. As he sensed unconsciousness drawing nearer and nearer, he prayed; not asking God why, but instead asking for forgiveness and giving thanks. He knew in his heart now that God's will couldn't be broken and that all things happen in life for a reason. He prayed for his family and that they would understand how much he loved them. He prayed that they would come into a relationship with God like he had come to love and appreciate in the past couple of days.

He finished his prayer and opened his eyes to a world that had become blurry. He could just barely make out shapes of trees and rocks. His mouth was dry, he realized, as his hands fumbled for the canteen that was strapped to the side of his pack, something was wrong. His hands weren't working right. He couldn't seem to grasp the canvas-covered water container. For a moment he watched in amazement as his hand would not do what he intended. He felt as if he were in a slow-motion picture, like a bad dream from which he couldn't awaken. This would be the conclusion to his life then, he reasoned, with what was left of his conscious abilities. Everything he'd lived for—his thoughts, hopes, and dreams—would end here.

He thought of all of the times that he had strived to get ahead in the business world. They were meaningless days, he now knew. Yet the important things he had left unattended. He had left his wife to raise their two children. He hadn't spent the time he should have with them for some time because of his job. All the time he thought he was climbing a mountain of success, but instead he was digging a hole for himself. He had been so wrapped up in self-importance that he couldn't see what was good for his soul. Now he was ready to go home and could feel death knocking at his door. He felt the cold of the snow against his face and couldn't remember falling over. He didn't have the strength or the desire to rise anymore, but he wasn't mad. God had given and given generously to him over the years. He had abused the gifts, and they were taken away. Such is life; all things pass away. Health comes and goes just as wealth and influence. The only true thing left is the soul. Matthew vaguely became aware of everything turning gray as he opened his eyes a fraction. There were no colors anymore. The greens and browns of the trees were all a darker or lighter shade of gray. There was no pain anymore, as the nerve endings in his body began to shut down.

He must have passed then. It was strange; not at all what he had been prepared for. Death appeared much like slipping off to sleep. He never had really considered what it might be like when someone crossed over and passed away from this life. He felt as though he were being swept up into a windstorm. The cold wind began engulfing him and taking him in into its midst. Then there were the hands on him and the distant voices. Inaudible voices that seemed to be coming from still another place in time. A thumping sound all too familiar began penetrating his mind. At first it was weak, as if from some great distance, and then louder; louder still. He couldn't remember where he had heard it before, but out of the depths of his conscious psyche, he began to pull up an image just as he felt himself being lifted up. Higher and higher his body floated and then suddenly jarred to a stop. An angelic voice reached him in that instant, a voice that at first he could not recognize. It was Kate! He was confused at first. *How could she be here,* he thought?

His eyes flittered open ever so slightly. He could just make out the outline of her leaning over him and sobbing hysterically. Her words were muffled. Again he felt himself being lifted, and in the background he could here voices, voices that echoed and crackled with static like a radio transmission. The thumping noise made sense now as he grasped what the sound really was. It had to be, a helicopter's rotors. He tried to smile, and for the first time Kate saw the signs of life in him. She began to call out, "He's alive!"

Another face came into view, although it held no recognition for Matt. He could hear the excitability in Kate's voice in the background. He tried to speak, but it was useless. His mouth and his brain seemed to be on different pages. He thought about what had happened. He'd put himself out on the face of that mountain in the midst of a terrible winter storm. There wasn't much chance for survival in those circumstances. He'd given up, ready to die, and God had said, "Not yet!"

He'd been prepared to face death several times in the last few days, and his creator had intervened. It wasn't his time, Matthew realized. God's will had been done. There were some tough days ahead for him, this he knew. But he also knew he had become a better man, a man seasoned with the Holy Spirit, and tried on a cold hard mountain; He had no idea where his road would lead. God would direct his path. Each step would be one taken in faith. A new lease on life had been given to him and Matthew knew he needed to make the most of it. His journey in the past had always been about himself, always taking more than he had given. In the future, his road would no longer be for the glory of Matthew, but instead, *for the glory of God.*